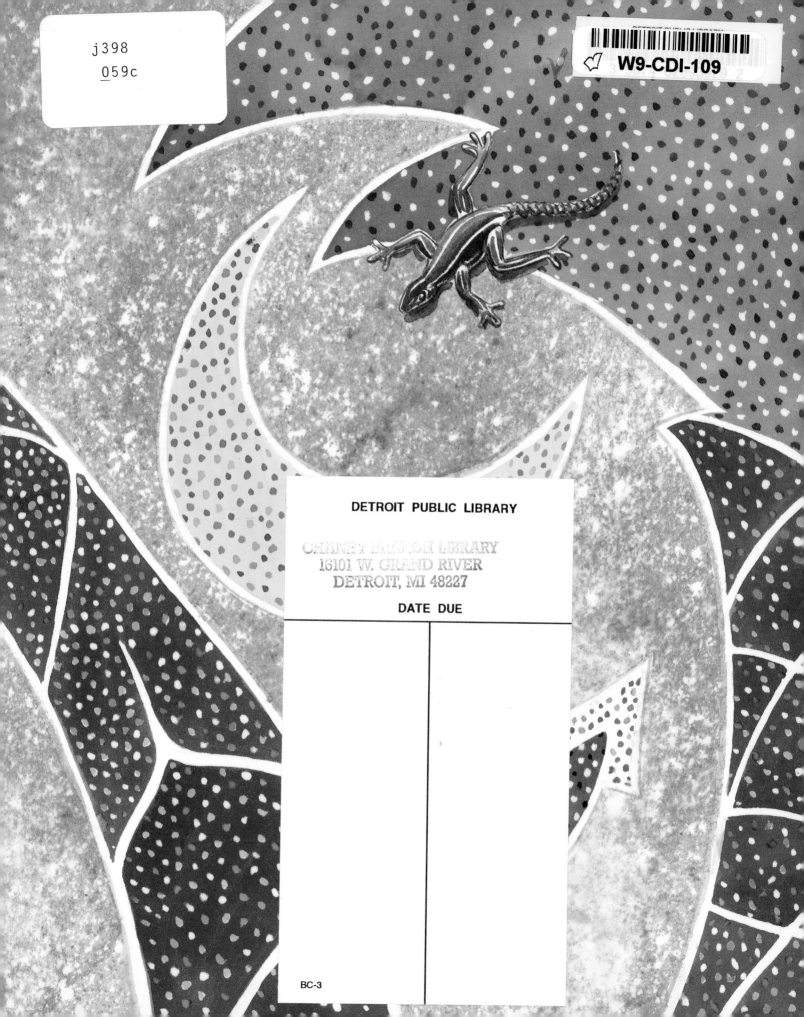

To my mother Emily Nkemjika,
my sisters Ifeoma and Chinye,
and to my daughter Emily Nkiruka – O.O.

VIKING
Published by the Penguin Group
Penguin Books USA Inc., 375 Hudson Street, New York, New York 10014, U.S.A.
Penguin Books Ltd, 27 Wrights Lane, London W8 5TZ, England
Penguin Books Australia Ltd, Ringwood, Victoria, Australia
Penguin Books Canada Ltd, 10 Alcorn Avenue, Toronto, Ontario, Canada M4V 3B2
Penguin Books (N.Z.) Ltd, 182–190 Wairau Road, Auckland 10, New Zealand

Penguin Books Ltd, Registered Offices: Harmondsworth, Middlesex, England

First published in Great Britain by Frances Lincoln Limited, 1994
4 Torriano Mews, Torriano Avenue, London NW5 2RZ

First published in the United States of America by Viking,
a division of Penguin Books USA Inc., 1994

1 3 5 7 9 10 8 6 4 2

Text copyright © Obi Onyefulu, 1994
Illustrations copyright © Evie Safarewicz, 1994
All rights reserved
Library of Congress Catalog Card Number 93-60837
ISBN 0-670-85115-9
Printed in Hong Kong
Set in Palatino

CHINYE
A WEST AFRICAN FOLK TALE

RETOLD BY OBI ONYEFULU
ILLUSTRATED BY EVIE SAFAREWICZ

VIKING

Long ago there lived a girl called Chinye. Her mother and father were dead, so she lived with her stepmother, Nkechi, and her stepsister, Adanma.

Every day Nkechi made Chinye do all the work and sent her back and forth through the forest to fetch water. Chinye was a quiet, obedient girl, and she worked as hard as she could to please Nkechi. She got no help from Adanma, who was spoiled and lazy.

One night, there was no water in the house to cook supper. Adanma had used all of it for a bath. But it was no good trying to explain this to Nkechi.

"Go to the stream at once and get more water, you bad girl," she shouted angrily.

To reach the stream, Chinye had to go through the forest. Wild animals prowled there, and even on moonlit nights the bravest villagers stayed at home. Chinye begged Nkechi to let her borrow water from a neighbor instead. It was no good.

"Be off with you!" Nkechi shouted, thrusting the heavy waterpot into Chinye's arms.

Weeping, Chinye set off into the forest. Danger lurked behind every tree. A lion roared, and her heart jumped.

Then, right in front of her, a shape loomed up on the path. Chinye screamed. Too terrified to run, she shut her eyes and prayed.

"Where are you going, child?" asked a gentle voice. Chinye opened her eyes in wonder. By the light of the moon, the shape looked like an antelope.

"To the stream, to fetch water," she whispered.

"The forest is no place for you at this time of night," the voice said. "Go home."

Chinye shook her head. "I can't. My life is bad enough already, without making my stepmother angry!"

The shape sighed and let Chinye pass.

A little further on, a second shape appeared. This one looked like a hyena. Once again Chinye screamed and shut her eyes, but the creature's voice was full of love and kindness. Hearing why Chinye was out so late, it said: "Go on your way with my blessing. But take care— a lion is following me. Hide behind this tree and wait until it has passed."

When the lion had gone, Chinye crept out from behind the tree and hurried on toward the stream. She hastily filled her waterpot, then ran back the way she had come.

Suddenly, right in front of her she saw an old woman, bent with age.

"Bless you, child," she told Chinye, reaching out as if to hold her. "Listen to me. As you go on your way, you will pass a hut and hear the sound of drums and singing. Go in, and you will find the floor of the hut covered with gourds—some big, some small, some quiet, some noisy. One of them will call to you, 'Take me!' but do not take it: it is full of evil things. Choose the smallest, quietest gourd, and when you get home, break it open on the ground."

The old woman blessed her again, and disappeared.

Sure enough, in a little while Chinye heard
the sound of drums and singing, and there
by the path, in the moonlight, stood a hut
she had never seen before. Chinye lowered
her waterpot carefully to the ground and went in.

Everything was just as the old woman had said.
Gourds of every shape and size covered the floor,
and from one of them a voice cried, "Take me!"
but Chinye remembered the old woman's warning.
She searched until she found the smallest, quietest
gourd and took that instead.

Once more the figure of the old woman appeared.
"You have chosen wisely," she said. "Make good
use of whatever fortune brings you." She stretched out
a hand and touched Chinye tenderly on the cheek.
"Now, go home in peace, my child."

Nkechi was waiting at the door of their hut.

   "What took you so long?" she demanded, glaring.
"And what's that in your hand?" She pointed
suspiciously at the gourd Chinye was carrying.
"An old woman gave it to you? What's inside?"

   She snatched the gourd and rattled it violently,
but it made no sound and she tossed it aside.

   "Hurry up and build a fire. We've waited long
enough for food tonight," she shouted.

   So there was no chance for Chinye to break open
the gourd that night.

Next morning, Chinye awoke early. Nkechi
and Adanma were fast asleep. Chinye found
the gourd and crept out to her father's old hut,
then locked the door and smashed the gourd
on the ground.

At a stroke the bare hut was transformed into
a treasure-house: gold ornaments spilled across
the floor, mingled with ivory and swaths of
rare damask in all the colors under the sun.
Chinye rubbed her eyes. Then she ran to wake
her stepmother.

When Nkechi saw the treasure, for once in her life she was speechless. To think that such treasure had come from a gourd! Why couldn't it have been Adanma who met the old woman?

Aha! Nkechi's eyes gleamed greedily. Maybe it was not too late!

That very night Nkechi carried out her plan, and sent Adanma down to the stream to fill the pot. Like Chinye, Adanma met the antelope, the hyena, and the old woman. But unlike Chinye, she paid no attention to the old woman's advice, and when she came to the hut and heard one of the biggest gourds say, "Take me!" she did just that.

Look, Mother," she said proudly when she got home. "I chose the biggest gourd I could!"

Nkechi rubbed her hands: the bigger the gourd, the greater the treasure. And with a cry of "We're rich! We're rich!" she snatched the gourd from Adanma and dashed it to the floor.

There was a flash of light and a clap of thunder. Nkechi and Adanma screamed and clutched each other. A great whirlwind sprang up, gathered all their belongings, and flung them out through the window— pots, pans, clothes, and cowrie shells were swept away into the night. Nkechi and Adanma had lost everything.

Too proud to ask Chinye for help, Nkechi left the village forever, taking Adanma with her.

And Chinye? She used her wealth to help the people of her village and lived happily ever after.